The Three Musketeers

Rebecca Levene
Based on the novel by Alexander Dumas

Illustrated by Victor Tavares

Reading Consultant: Alison Kelly
Roehampton University

Designed by Michelle Lawrence
Series designer: Russell Punter
Series editor: Lesley Sims

Internet Links

To find out more about fencing, Musketeer-style,
and to explore a French palace, go to the Usborne
Quicklinks Website at www.usborne-quicklinks.com.
Read the internet safety guidelines, and then
type the keyword "Musketeers".

First published in 2009 by Usborne Publishing Ltd., Usborne House,
83-85 Saffron Hill, London EC1N 8RT, England. www.usborne.com
Copyright © 2009 Usborne Publishing Ltd.

Contents

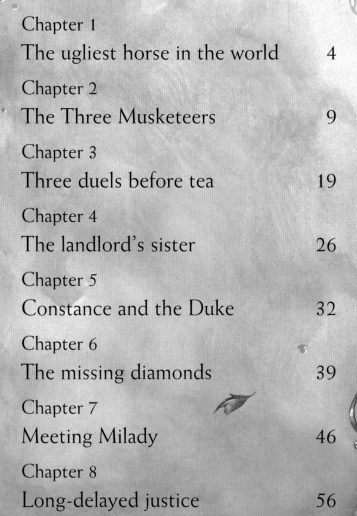

Chapter 1

The ugliest horse in the world

When d'Artagnan left home, his father gave him three things: 15 gold coins, a letter of introduction to the captain of the musketeers in Paris, and a remarkably ugly yellow horse.

Everywhere d'Artagnan went, people noticed his horse. Then they noticed a sword hanging from his belt and decided to keep their thoughts to themselves.

Just outside Paris, d'Artagnan came to a little pub called the Jolly Miller and met a man who couldn't help laughing at the ridiculous animal.

"Have you seen that creature?" the man guffawed to his friends. "It's as yellow as a buttercup!"

D'Artagnan was young and proud and he couldn't let an insult go unchallenged. "Mock my horse," he snarled, "and you mock me. I challenge you to a duel, sir!"

The stranger laughed and, for the first time, d'Artagnan noticed a ragged scar which ran the length of his cheek.

"A duel?" he scoffed. "Surely you know that the King has banned them."

D'Artagnan wouldn't be put off. He drew his sword and lunged for the man. The stranger quickly pulled out his own sword, but before the fight could begin, d'Artagnan felt something heavy hit the back of his head. Desperate to stop the fight, the barman had knocked him out.

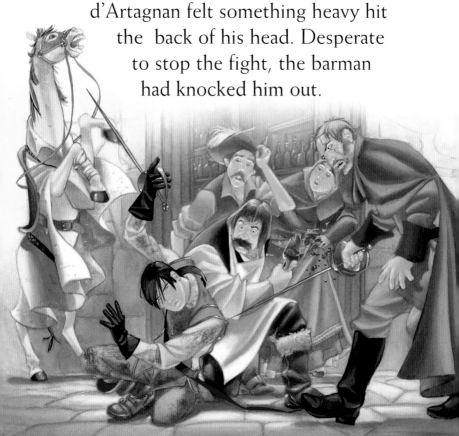

When d'Artagnan woke, his head throbbed painfully. He looked around and saw the scarred man talking to a woman inside a horse-drawn carriage.

"You must go back to England, Milady de Winter," the scarred man told the woman. "Inform the Cardinal as soon as the Duke leaves London."

The man spurred his horse and, before d'Artagnan could stop him, he'd galloped into the distance. "Blast him!" d'Artagnan cried. "Now I shall never avenge his insult!"

His voice died out as he got a close look at Milady's face. She had golden hair, huge blue eyes and rose-red lips, and d'Artagnan thought she was the most beautiful woman he'd ever seen.

"Milady," he said. For one moment her eyes met his – then she gave a quiet command and the carriage sped off into the distance. D'Artagnan stared after it, wondering if he would ever see her again.

Chapter 2

The Three Musketeers

The following day, d'Artagnan was in Paris, his eyes wide as he rode through the streets. He'd never seen a city so grand, bustling with people and lined with imposing houses built from golden stone.

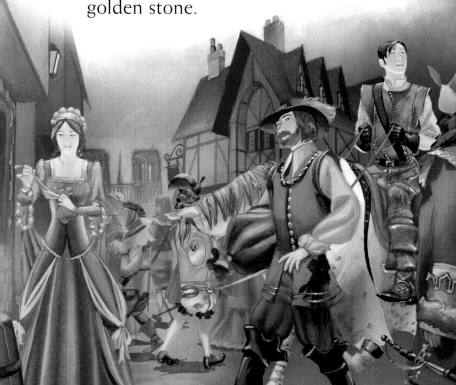

Soon he was at the house of Mr. de Treville, the captain of the King's musketeers, the most famous soldiers in France. For as long as he could remember, d'Artagnan had wanted nothing more than to serve in that élite force.

"Mr. de Treville might be able to spare you a few minutes," said the servant who answered the door, sniffing disapprovingly as he studied d'Artagnan's shabby clothes.

D'Artagnan swallowed nervously, but he held his head high as he walked into the room. Mr. de Treville was wearing a frown so fierce it could have curdled milk. He ignored d'Artagnan completely and instead bellowed, "Athos! Porthos! Aramis! Come in and see me at once!"

Two men rushed into the room. Porthos was tall with a long black moustache and an even longer nose, which he gazed down at everyone around him. Aramis was smaller and thinner and his face was as innocent as a child's.

"I hear you've been duelling with the Cardinal's guards," de Treville snapped. "And worse than that – you lost! What do you have to say for yourselves?"

"It's true we were defeated," Aramis said indignantly, "but that's because we were outnumbered and taken by surprise."

"Athos was very badly injured," Porthos explained, as a third musketeer entered.

Athos was older than his two friends and would have been strikingly handsome if he hadn't been so pale. "Nonsense!" he declared. "It was just a scratch." But his lips were thin with pain.

"I suppose you did your best," de Treville said reluctantly. "Just don't get caught like that again." The three musketeers bowed and left. "And what do you want?" de Treville asked d'Artagnan, seeming to notice him for the first time.

"I want to join the musketeers," d'Artagnan declared, though inside he was filled with uncertainty. How could he ever match up to the men he'd just seen?

De Treville seemed to feel the same. "An inexperienced boy like you join the most famous regiment in France?" he scoffed. "No, if you want to become a musketeer, you must first prove yourself worthy of our uniform."

Just then, d'Artagnan glimpsed a man out of de Treville's window. It was the scarred stranger who had laughed at his horse. Without even calling good-bye, d'Artagnan ran out after the man.

D'Artagnan was moving so fast, and his attention was fixed so firmly on the stranger, that he didn't see Athos until he'd bumped right into him.

"Watch it, you fool!" shouted Athos.

"Who are you calling a fool?" d'Artagnan said indignantly. "You're the one in the way."

"I'm not a man to take an insult lying down." Athos spoke haughtily, though his hand was clutched to his side in pain. "I demand that you meet me by the deserted monastery for a duel at noon tomorrow."

All d'Artagnan could think of was the man with the scar, who was in danger of disappearing into the crowd. "Fine," he said. "Tomorrow I'll teach you some manners." Then he ran off, eyes still fixed on the man he was pursuing rather than the people around him.

This time it was Porthos who stood in
his way. D'Artagnan found himself tangled
in the other man's magnificent cloak
– revealing the threadbare clothes Porthos
was wearing underneath.

"You young whippersnapper!" Porthos
bellowed. "You've made me look ridiculous.
I demand satisfaction. We'll cross swords at
the deserted monastery at one tomorrow."

D'Artagnan didn't even answer. He
simply nodded and carried on running after
the stranger. It was no use; the other
man had made good his escape.

"Bother!" d'Artagnan exclaimed. "I've lost my quarry and offended two strangers. I really must try to be more civil in future."

So when he passed Aramis, d'Artagnan decided to be as friendly as possible. "Sir, it appears you've dropped something," he said, picking up a handkerchief from the ground beside Aramis.

Aramis was furious. The handkerchief had been given to him by a female admirer, and he'd been hoping to keep it secret. "Interfere in my business, will you!" he snapped at d'Artagnan. "I'll soon teach you better – when I defeat you in a duel at two o'clock tomorrow. Be waiting at the deserted monastery."

Shoulders slumped, d'Artagnan slunk back to his lodgings. He'd come to Paris to make his fortune, and instead he'd made three deadly new enemies.

Chapter 3

Three duels before tea

"Are you alone?" Athos asked d'Artagnan, when the two men met the following day. "It hardly seems right to kill a man who doesn't have a friend in the world."

"I'm the one who should feel guilty," said d'Artagnan, "for fighting a duel with an injured man."

It was true that Athos didn't look well. His face was as white as the clouds scudding across the sky, and his arm was clutched to his wounded side.

"I tell you what," d'Artagnan offered. "Why don't I let you have some of my mother's special ointment? You can put it on your wounds and when you're feeling better we'll meet again for our duel."

Athos was impressed with his gallantry. "That's very noble, sir, but even injured as I am, you won't find me an easy match."

D'Artagnan bowed and drew his sword. Before the duel could begin, two more men arrived: Porthos and Aramis.

"You're early!" d'Artagnan exclaimed. "It's an hour before I'm due to fight Porthos and another two hours until I'm meeting Aramis."

"Hold on!" Athos said. "You've both arranged duels with this man?"

"So it would appear," Porthos said. "He must be a very hot-tempered fellow."

"Well, when I'm through with him, I'm afraid there won't be much left for you two to fight," Athos said.

He lunged towards d'Artagnan and their swords met with a metallic clang.

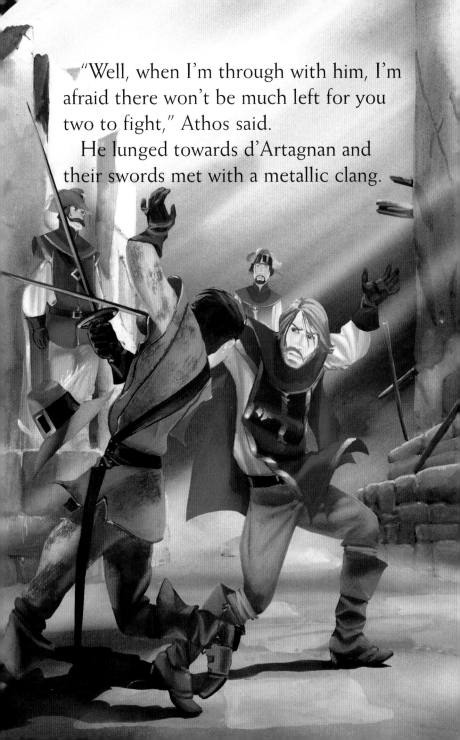

"Halt!" a voice shouted. "Duels are against the law!" It was the Cardinal's guards. Soldiers of the Cardinal, the King's right-hand man, they despised the musketeers and were delighted to have found an excuse to arrest one.

"You're not taking Athos without a fight," Porthos declared, as he and Aramis drew their own swords.

D'Artagnan looked between the groups: the Cardinal's guards, who had probably just saved his life, and the musketeers who had been planning to take it.

"If there's going to be a fight," he said, "there's only one side I can take – the King's musketeers!" He flourished his sword as he went to stand beside Athos, Porthos and Aramis.

There were five guards and four of them, but d'Artagnan was fighting beside three of the finest swordsmen in the land.

Aramis struck, faster than lightning, and thrust his sword into his opponent's heart. Another guard cried out as Porthos plunged his blade through his leg.

Athos fought hard as well, but his wound slowed him down. D'Artagnan leaped forward, putting his own body between a guard's sword and Athos's chest. In a second he'd disarmed the guard and rescued Athos.

The fight was over. D'Artagnan and the three musketeers were on their feet, but all five guards lay on the ground.

Athos turned to smile at d'Artagnan. "I think I shall have to call off our duel. It doesn't seem right to kill a man who's just saved my life."

Aramis and Porthos nodded their agreement.

"It was a privilege to fight by your side," d'Artagnan said, bowing. "From now on, we should always stick together. One for all, and all for one, that's what I say."

The three musketeers liked this new motto very much. "All for one," they chorused, "and one for all!"

Chapter 4

The landlord's sister

Over the next few weeks, d'Artagnan tried to find out more about his new friends. Aramis, he discovered, dreamed of being a priest rather than a fighter. Porthos cared about nothing but beautiful clothes and beautiful women. He spent his free time chasing after rich widows.

Athos, however, remained an enigma. He never laughed and seldom smiled. Sometimes, d'Artagnan thought he detected a deep sadness in his companion, but whenever he asked Athos about it, the other man would shrug and change the subject.

D'Artagnan was still pondering the secret of his friend's past when he heard a knock on his door. It was his landlord, a short man with a high opinion of himself.

"Oh, Mr. d'Artagnan!" he said, walking
into the house without being invited.
"Something awful has happened and
you're the only one I can turn to. My
sister Constance has been kidnapped!"

"Why would anyone want to kidnap
your sister?" d'Artagnan asked.

"She works for the Queen," his landlord
explained. "And the Queen has powerful
enemies. They hope to prise the Queen's
secrets from my poor sister."

"That is terrible," d'Artagnan agreed.
"As a musketeer – or at least a musketeer
in training – I'm bound to protect the
royal family. Do you know who took her?"

"I don't know his name but I'll never
forget his face," said his landlord. "He has
a scar running the length of his cheek."

"That man!" d'Artagnan exclaimed.

"I think he's one of the Cardinal's
agents," his landlord went on. "It's well-
known that the Cardinal hates the Queen.
I'm sure he's behind this."

D'Artagnan prowled the streets of Paris searching for Constance, but she seemed to have vanished completely. After a fourth day of fruitless searching, he returned miserably to his house. Before he could enter, he noticed a light shining next door. It was his landlord's house — but he knew his landlord was out searching for his sister.

D'Artagnan drew his sword from its scabbard, then flung the door open.

Inside, he was amazed to see a young woman, no older than himself. Her hair was blonde, her face was soft and he thought that she was very pretty.

"What are you doing here?" he asked uncertainly, lowering his sword.

"What are you doing here?" she retorted. "This is my brother's house."

D'Artagnan realized in amazement that he'd found Constance.

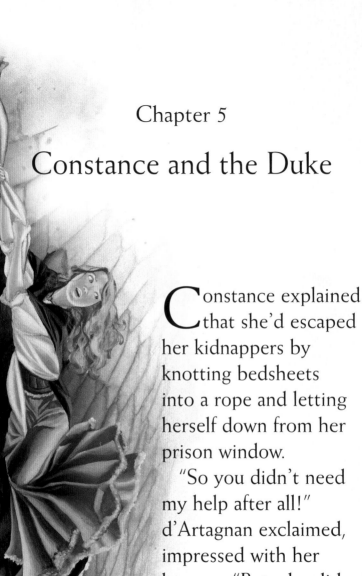

Chapter 5

Constance and the Duke

Constance explained that she'd escaped her kidnappers by knotting bedsheets into a rope and letting herself down from her prison window.

"So you didn't need my help after all!" d'Artagnan exclaimed, impressed with her bravery. "But why did they kidnap you?"

"That is someone else's secret," said Constance. "I can't reveal it to you. And now I'm afraid I must go."

D'Artagnan didn't want to let this intriguing young woman leave. "The people you escaped may still be chasing you," he said. "Let me guard you."

Constance refused and left the house before d'Artagnan could argue.

Still, he decided that he had better make sure she was safe. He crept after her along the quiet, late night streets of Paris, sticking to the shadows so she wouldn't know he was following.

Eventually she came to one of the many bridges crossing the river. She had just stepped onto it, when a man approached her from behind and grabbed her shoulder.

"Let go of her!" d'Artagnan roared, leaping out and tearing the man's hand away from Constance.

"D'Artagnan!" she said angrily. "What are you doing here? I told you not to follow me."

"I thought you might need protection and I was right," he said, glaring at the man.

Constance sighed. "This man isn't my enemy," she explained. "He's the Duke of Buckingham. I was sent here to meet him by the Queen."

"But why would she want you to meet an English nobleman?" d'Artagnan asked.

"Because the Queen loves me and I love her," said the Duke.

Like all good Frenchmen, d'Artagnan hated the English, but this man seemed an honest, likeable person.

"I came to France in secret to see the Queen," the Duke continued, "but Constance tells me that the Cardinal's agents are hunting for me. They'll kill me if they find me."

"Then I shall guard you both," declared d'Artagnan. "No one will dare to attack you with me by your side."

D'Artagnan was as good as his word, and got them safely into the palace.

As soon as he saw the Queen, the Duke took her in his arms. "Oh, I've missed you!" he said.

Although the Queen didn't love the King, having been forced to marry him when she was very young, she knew she had to keep her wedding vows. "Please return to England," she begged the Duke. "We can never be together... but take this as a token of my love." And she handed the Duke a beautiful rosewood box. Inside were twelve diamonds on a ribbon, a present to her from the King.

What the Queen didn't realize was that someone else was watching. A man with a scarred face stood in the shadows, smiling. He saw the Queen hand over the diamonds, then ran to tell the Cardinal.

The next day, the Cardinal suggested the King hold a ball for the Queen. "Tell her to wear the diamonds."

The Queen turned pale when she heard. "Somehow he must have found out that I've given them away."

"Don't despair, your Majesty," said Constance. "I'll ask d'Artagnan to go to England and fetch them."

She found him at duelling practice. When d'Artagnan saw Constance again, he thought she looked even prettier than he remembered. He agreed to her plan at once. He might not survive the trip, but it would be worth the risk if it meant Constance fell in love with him.

Chapter 6

The missing diamonds

D'Artagnan told his three friends about the mission and they insisted on coming along. "Remember," Athos told him. "It's all for one and one for all."

Unluckily for them, the Cardinal had discovered the plan, and he was determined to do everything in his power to stop d'Artagnan from reaching England.

Porthos was the first to fall foul of the Cardinal's plotting. In a small inn on the outskirts of Paris, an agent of the Cardinal provoked him into a fight. Porthos won the duel, but he didn't escape unscathed. Reluctantly, d'Artagnan left his friend behind to recover from his wounds.

D'Artagnan, Athos and Aramis rode on into the night, but the danger was far from over. The Cardinal had organized an ambush on the road that led to the coast.

D'Artagnan and Athos galloped through as arrows rained around them, but Aramis was thrown from his horse. D'Artagnan wanted to stay and help him, but he'd made a promise to the Queen. With a heavy heart, he spurred his horse on.

When they reached the coast, they stopped at an inn overnight. But the innkeeper too was the Cardinal's agent, and, while d'Artagnan slept, he imprisoned Athos in his cellar.

D'Artagnan searched the inn, but he couldn't find Athos anywhere and there was no more time to waste. Sighing, he paid his passage and boarded the first ship bound for England – completely alone as he sailed to a dangerous foreign land.

The crossing was stormy and the English were unwelcoming, but d'Artagnan didn't let that put him off. He was determined to save the Queen.

D'Artagnan finally found the Duke hunting in the countryside with the English King. "Your Grace," he called, as he leaped off his horse. "I bring a message from the Queen of France. She needs you to return her diamonds. Without them, she'll be disgraced."

The Duke looked sick.

"Oh no," he said. "I've kept them in the box but when I last looked, two were missing."

"You've lost them?" yelled d'Artagnan.

"No." The Duke shook his head. "I believe they were stolen by Milady de Winter, an agent of the Cardinal's who lives in London."

As he described Milady, d'Artagnan realized that it was the very same woman he'd seen talking to the man with the scar, in the carriage all those weeks ago.

"Well, I can't return to France without the diamonds," d'Artagnan told the Duke. "Constance will never forgive me."

"Don't panic," said the Duke firmly. "I'll hire the best goldsmith in the land to cut and polish two new ones. No one will be able to tell the difference."

Three days later, the Duke had twelve diamonds once again. "Here," he said, giving them to d'Artagnan. "I only hope it's not too late."

D'Artagnan rode his horse so fast, the poor animal almost collapsed. Then he took the swiftest ship he could find. He stood in the prow as it crossed the waters, as if he could will the wind to fill its sails.

Finally, he raced back into Paris just as the ball was about to begin.

The Queen was in despair. As soon as she saw d'Artagnan with the diamonds, her face broke into a huge smile. "You did it!" she cried.

"I would do anything to serve you, your Majesty," d'Artagnan said, but he was looking at Constance as he said it.

Chapter 7

Meeting Milady

A few days later, d'Artagnan received a note from Constance. "Come and meet me at the summerhouse outside the city," it read. She wanted to see him! D'Artagnan was delighted.

He rode to the summerhouse at once. But when he arrived, he found it ransacked. Chairs were broken, books were scattered all over the floor – and there was no sign of Constance.

Desperately, he asked people living nearby if they had seen what happened.

"It was a man with a scar," a woman told him. "We saw him carrying Constance away, kicking and screaming."

"The Cardinal's agent," d'Artagnan thought bitterly. "He's taken Constance because we helped the Queen."

D'Artagnan tore back to the city to beg his friends for help.

"This is what happens when you fall in love," said Athos. "Women were put on earth to bring misery into our lives."

Porthos laughed. "Nonsense! Besides, what would you know about it? I've never even seen you speak to a woman."

"I was married once," Athos said quietly. "She was the love of my life. But after our wedding I saw a flower-shaped scar on her shoulder, the brand of a common criminal. She'd been caught stealing from the Church. I threw her out of my house. I've not let myself love another woman since."

Still, he agreed to help d'Artagnan hunt
for Constance. The four men searched
all of Paris and outside the city too. They
spoke to her brother and they asked
the Queen, but no one knew where
Constance was.

Walking home in despair, d'Artagnan
spotted a head of golden hair in the
crowd. She turned – and he recognized
Milady de Winter.

"She works for the Cardinal too,"
d'Artagnan muttered to himself. "She
must know where Constance is."

The next day, he presented himself
at Milady's house, dressed in his finest
clothes. "I've come to pay court to
the most beautiful woman in France,"
he declared.

He wasn't alone. D'Artagnan found out that many men were pursuing Milady, though she seemed to like just one, a sour-faced nobleman called the Count of Wardes. She was polite to d'Artagnan, but he sensed distrust lurking behind her wide smile.

"She sounds dangerous," Athos had said. "You should stay away from her."

But d'Artagnan was sure she was his only hope of finding Constance. Day after day, he returned to pay her compliments – until he had a piece of luck. He intercepted a letter Milady had written to the Count of Wardes, asking him to meet her in secret later that night.

Milady never guessed that the man behind the curtain was d'Artagnan and not the Count.

"Thank goodness you've come," she said, sounding sweeter than she ever had when she spoke to d'Artagnan. "I've been having the most miserable week!"

"Why is that?" asked d'Artagnan, speaking softly to disguise his voice.

"That dreadful d'Artagnan has been visiting me every day," she said. "How I loathe that man."

"You do?" D'Artagnan was puzzled.

"He ruined all my plans," Milady replied. "Thanks to him, I nearly lost my position with the Cardinal. He's an interfering, arrogant, strutting young fool!"

This was too much for d'Artagnan, who leaped from behind the curtain. "Not such a fool that I can't trick you!"

Milady backed away in horror.

"Now tell me where Constance is," d'Artagnan demanded.

"Your little damsel in distress? The Cardinal asked me to send her somewhere you'll never find," she sneered. She pulled a knife from beneath her bodice and lunged for him.

D'Artagnan grabbed her arm to stop her.
The knife clattered to the floor and her
dress ripped beneath his hand. Underneath
it, her shoulder was marked with a brand
in the shape of a flower.

Milady pulled herself from his grasp and
scrambled from the room.

D'Artagnan was too startled to move.
Milady was a common criminal – and she
was branded in the same place as Athos's
long-lost wife.

Chapter 8

Long-delayed justice

Athos was shocked to discover that the woman who had helped to kidnap Constance might be the same criminal he had once married.

He helped d'Artagnan break into Milady's house to search for clues. Athos paused, a wistful expression on his face, when he found an antique ring in a cabinet. "This was a family heirloom," he said. "I gave it to her on our wedding day."

At last, they found what they were looking for – a letter arranging for Constance to be held in a convent.

"Don't worry d'Artagnan," Athos reassured him. "We'll get Porthos and Aramis and rescue her."

The convent lay many miles outside Paris, and even on the fastest horses the journey took hours. D'Artagnan and his three friends rode through the night, desperate to rescue Constance.

But when the convent finally loomed in front of them, they saw Milady's carriage outside, its open door creaking in the wind.

Inside, Milady was speaking to
Constance. "I'm a friend of d'Artagnan's.
He sent me to rescue you."

There was something about the other
woman that Constance didn't trust.
"Why didn't d'Artagnan come himself?"
she asked.

Milady smiled sweetly. "Here,
drink a glass of wine with
me and I'll explain."

Constance took a glass from Milady. She hadn't noticed her sprinkle powder into it. She watched as Milady drank, then sipped the wine herself.

As soon as Constance's glass was empty, Milady smiled again, a vicious smile this time. "I think I hear d'Artagnan," she said, as the gate to the convent clanked open. "A shame you won't get to speak to him."

For a moment, Constance was confused. Then she felt a terrible heaviness spreading through her body and fell to the floor. "Have... you... poisoned me?" she choked.

Seconds later, d'Artagnan and the three musketeers rushed in. D'Artagnan fell to his knees beside Constance.

She looked at him, her face twisted with pain. "I love you," she whispered, as her eyes closed.

"I should have killed you when I had the chance," Athos told Milady bitterly. "You'll pay for this."

The four men took Milady outside and held a trial.

"The punishment should be death," d'Artagnan declared and she was executed. Justice had been served, but it wouldn't bring Constance back.

As soon as d'Artagnan set foot in Paris, he was summoned before the Cardinal. He assumed he was to be punished for what he had done to Milady.

Instead, the Cardinal said, "You're a brave, honest man, d'Artagnan. I'm very sorry that Constance was killed. Those were never my orders. I can't bring her back, but I can give you something else that you value." He handed d'Artagnan a piece of paper, stamped with his official seal. It was a commission to serve as a lieutenant in the King's musketeers.

D'Artagnan had finally achieved his dream. Alongside his three friends, he would serve his King proudly – the youngest of the Four Musketeers.

Alexander Dumas
1802-1870

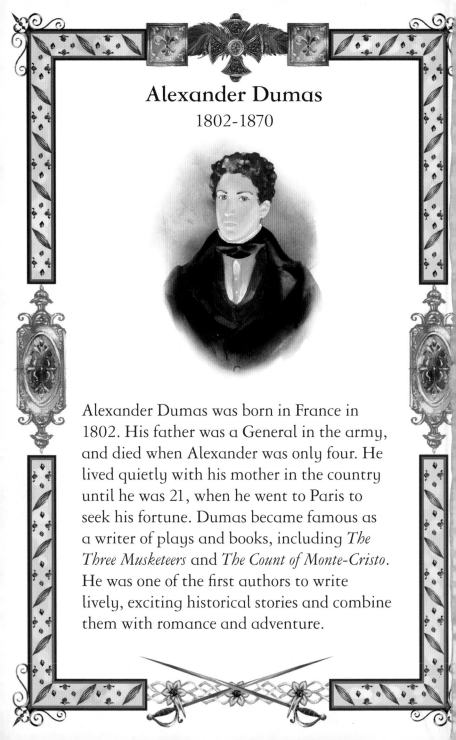

Alexander Dumas was born in France in 1802. His father was a General in the army, and died when Alexander was only four. He lived quietly with his mother in the country until he was 21, when he went to Paris to seek his fortune. Dumas became famous as a writer of plays and books, including *The Three Musketeers* and *The Count of Monte-Cristo*. He was one of the first authors to write lively, exciting historical stories and combine them with romance and adventure.